SHAHNAMEH FOR KIDS™

The Story of Zal & Simorgh

By Arsia Rozegar

Illustrated by Mike Amante

www.ShahnamehForKids.com

ISBN 978-0-692-57350-1
Kickstarter Edition

Printed in China

In honor of my Grandfather

Dedicated to Saba and Saghar

Special thanks to Mitra Daneshvar

Inspired by
Ferdowsi's Shahnameh

A long time ago, in the ancient Kingdom of **Sistan**, which was found in the land of **Greater Iran**, there was a noble by the name of **Saum**. Everyone admired and respected Saum because he was a good man with a pure heart.

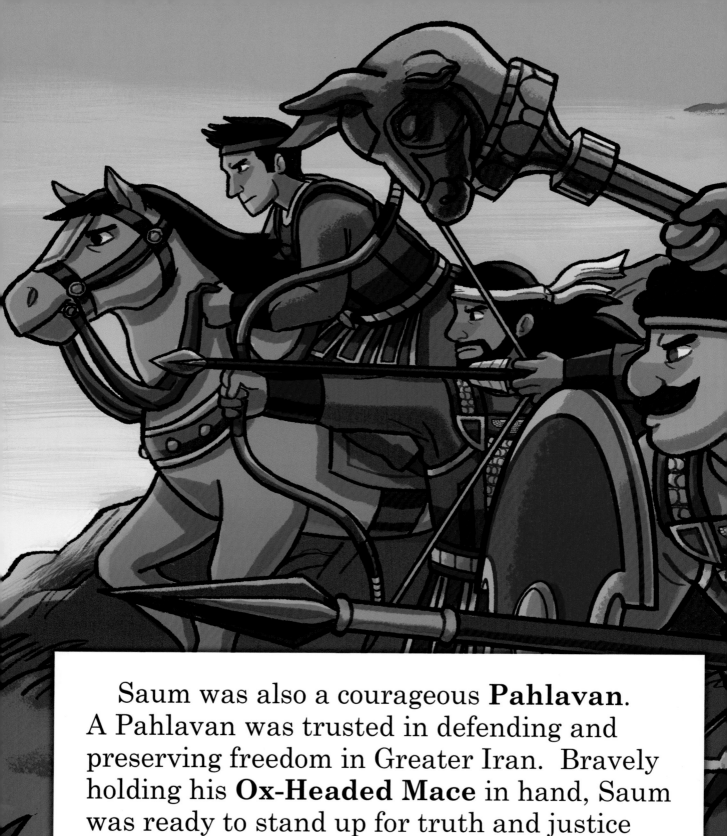

Saum was also a courageous **Pahlavan**. A Pahlavan was trusted in defending and preserving freedom in Greater Iran. Bravely holding his **Ox-Headed Mace** in hand, Saum was ready to stand up for truth and justice at all times.

Saum was even a very close personal friend of the great **Shah, Manuchehr**! The Shah ruled over all the kingdoms of Greater Iran and was responsible for the well-being and happiness of all its people.

It seemed like Saum had everything. However, there was one thing he did not have, and that was a child of his very own. One day, Saum's wife told him that she was expecting a baby. Saum was delighted to find out that he was going to be a father.

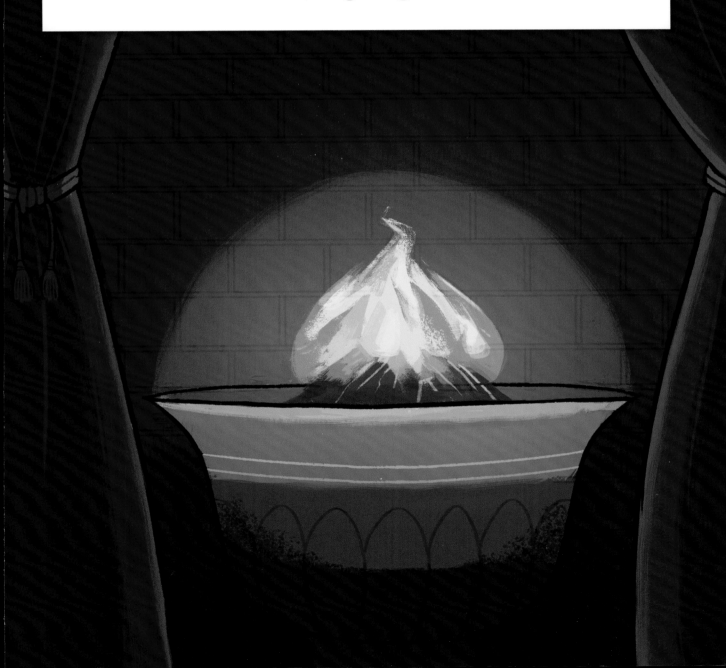

Many months later, the special day finally arrived and Saum recieved the news. His son was born and given the name **Zal**.

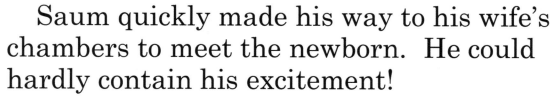

Saum quickly made his way to his wife's chambers to meet the newborn. He could hardly contain his excitement!

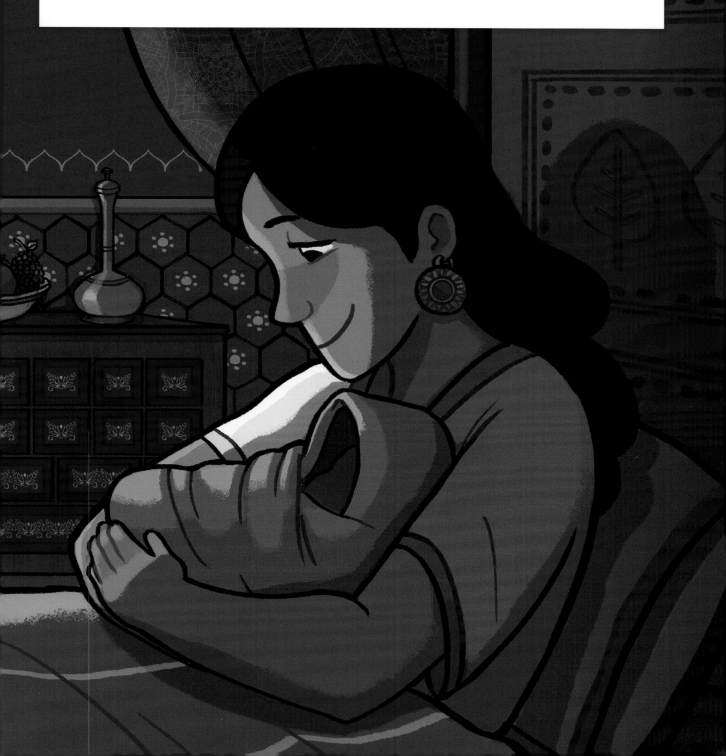

But as Saum laid eyes upon his son for the first time, he was shocked to see that Zal was born with skin and hair white as snow!

That night, alone in his chambers, Saum worried about what everyone would think of Zal's unusual appearance. What would his family and friends think? What would the Shah think?

Later, while the entire kingdom was fast asleep and no one was there to see, Saum took Zal with him on horseback, swiftly heading north towards the **Alborz Mountains**.

Saum hesitated as he placed Zal at the foot of **Mount Damavand**, the tallest mountain in all of Greater Iran.

With a heavy heart, Saum turned his back on his own son, leaving Zal all alone in the cold of night.

Several hours passed, and baby Zal grew cold and hungry. The little one cried out in anguish. Luckily, Zal's cries were heard by the mystical and magical giant bird known as **Simorgh**.

Simorgh took Zal to her nest high atop a mountian and raised him as if he was her very own.

Zal and Simorgh lived happily together, enjoying each moment, as days turned into weeks.

Weeks turned into months.

Months turned into years and in what seemed like no time at all, Zal grew up to be a tall, strong and confident young man.

On one particular day, a traveling caravan of merchants was taking a shortcut through the Alborz Mountains. They spotted Zal on a distant cliffside and were all extremely surprised to find a young man with such an unusual appearance, alone in the mountains.

When the caravan merchants arrived at the kingdom's bazaar, they told people all about what they witnessed on the way there. Everyone was fascinated by stories of a young man with skin and hair white as snow, living amongst the mountains.

Before long, Saum also heard the tale of a pale-skinned young man in the mountains. He knew exactly who that young man was. Saum had always felt shame and regret for abandoning his own son. Maybe now he could find Zal and make amends for what he did all those years ago.

Saum put together a search party to go out and find Zal. When they arrived at the Alborz Mountains, Simorgh saw them from a distance. She knew that they were there looking for Zal.

Simorgh flew back to the nest to tell Zal the news. "It is time for you to go back to your father and live amongst people," she said. Zal became sad and thought Simorgh did not love him anymore.

"I will always love you," Simorgh told Zal, "But there is nothing more for me to teach you and now is the beginning of a new chapter in your life. An amazing world is out there full of wonder and joy for you to experience." Simorgh then gave Zal three magical golden feathers and said, "If you ever need me, simply burn one of these feathers, and I will be there for you."

Meanwhile, at the foot of the mountain, Saum was rather upset. He realized that because of his old age and feeble bones, he was unable to climb up the rocky mountainside and search for Zal.

Suddenly, with the utmost grace and majesty, Simorgh descended from high above, firmly holding Zal. Saum was overjoyed to see his son again.

Saum was truly sorry for what he did all those years ago and apologized. Zal forgave him. Father and son were together again.

The entire kingdom celebrated Zal's return and a magnificent parade was held in his honor.

In time, Zal himself became a noble Pahlavan for Greater Iran. In addition to being brave, he was known for his loyalty, wisdom and good intentions.